The Big Wide-Mouthed Frog

A Traditional Tale

illustrated by

ANA MARTíN LARRAÑAGA

CANDLEWICK PRESS
CAMBRIDGE, MASSACHUSETTS

Once there was a big wide-mouthed frog with the biggest, widest mouth you ever did see.

And one day that
big wide-mouthed frog
hopped off to see the world.

The first creature he met had
big thumping feet.

"Hey, you! Big Thumping Feet!
Who are you, and what do you eat?"
shouted the wide-mouthed frog.
"I'm a kangaroo," said Kangaroo, "and I eat grass."
"Well, *I'm* a big wide-mouthed frog!"
shouted the wide-mouthed frog.
"And I eat flies!"

The second creature
he met had a big
black nose.

"Listen, Mr. Big Nose!
Who are you, and what do you eat?"
shouted the wide-mouthed frog.

"I'm a koala," said Koala,
"and I eat leaves."
"Well, *I'm* a big wide-mouthed frog!"
shouted the wide-mouthed frog.
"And I eat flies!"

The third
creature
he met
was
hanging
upside
down.

"Ho there,
Upside-down Creature!
Who are you, and what do you eat?"
shouted the wide-mouthed frog.
"I'm a possum," said Possum, "and I eat blossoms."
"Well, *I'm* a big wide-mouthed frog!"
shouted the wide-mouthed frog.
"And I eat flies!"

The fourth creature he met had three long toes. "Look here, Three Long Toes! Who are you, and what do you eat?" shouted the wide-mouthed frog.

"I'm an emu," said Emu, "and I eat grasshoppers."
"Well, *I'm* a big wide-mouthed frog!"
shouted the wide-mouthed frog.
"And I eat flies!"

Then the wide-mouthed frog met
a creature stretched out on the riverbank
like a knobby brown log.

"HEY, Knobby Brown Log!
Who are you, and what do you eat?"
shouted the wide-mouthed frog.

Knobby Brown Log opened her mouth
in a slow, wide, lazy smile.

"Good day to you, too," she said.
"I'm a crocodile, and I eat
big wide-mouthed frogs.
Who are you, and what do *you* eat?"

"*Me?*" whispered the wide-mouthed frog,
puckering his mouth into the smallest,
narrowest mouth you ever did see.

off!"

For Andrés

Text copyright © 1999 by Walker Books Ltd.
Illustrations copyright © 1999 by Ana Martín Larrañaga
Library of Congress Cataloging-in-Publication Data
Martín Larrañaga, Ana, date.
The big wide-mouthed frog / Ana Martín Larrañaga.—1st U.S. ed.
p. cm.
Summary: A big wide-mouthed frog asks every creature he meets what they like to eat,
but when he meets a crocodile he doesn't like the crocodile's answer.
ISBN 0-7636-0807-6 (hardcover).—ISBN 0-7636-0808-4 (paperback)
[1. Frogs—Fiction.]
PZ7.M3647Bi   1999
[E]—dc21   98-33873

10 9 8 7 6 5 4 3 2

Printed in Hong Kong

This book was typeset in Highlander Book.
The pictures were done in a variety of media including collage, gouache, and watercolor.

Candlewick Press, 2067 Massachusetts Avenue, Cambridge, Massachusetts 02140